C L A S S I C   T A I L S

Pugs & Prejudice

JANE AUSTEN
with ELIZA GARRETT

Illustrated by Bob Venables

WILDFIRE

It was Michaelmas, but that wasn't the only cause for celebration at Longbone. The eligible bachelor Mr Bingley had just moved to the grand Netherfield Bark estate in town, and it was all anyone could yip about.

There were four beautiful female pups in the Bennet household (plus a fifth, Kitty, who was a little odd – but no one could quite figure out why), and Mrs Bennet was eager to marry them off and secure their futures. 'A single pug in possession of a good fortune must be in want of a mate!' she squealed, and waggled her little curly tail. Legally, you see, the Bennets' kennel could only be inherited by a male heir.

Soon there was a ball (and there was nothing more beloved in the Bennet household than a ball). Bingley came, much to the town's delight, and was pronounced to be of most agreeable temperament, with perfect good breeding. His sisters and his friend, Mr Darcy, accompanied him.

Bingley took an immediate shine to Jane, the eldest Miss Bennet, and they spent the whole evening merrily frolicking about the ballroom. Darcy danced with no one – he was handsome of muzzle and glossy of coat, but far too proud.

Bingley enquired whether Darcy wanted to dance with Elizabeth, the second Miss Bennet.

'She is not handsome enough to tempt *me*,' he sniffed haughtily.

Elizabeth, overhearing, chortled to herself. She didn't care – for there was a more honourable and gentle pug at the ball: the charming army officer Mr Wickham. Darcy seemed to detest Wickham, which was even more of a treat.

Soon after the ball, Jane was invited to Bingley's Netherfield mansion, but caught terrible sniffles in the rain on her way there. She had no choice but to stay a few days to recover (much to Mrs Bennet's delight).

Elizabeth, however, was concerned for poor Jane, and went for brisk walkies through the mud to be with her. The Bingley sisters were scandalized by her impropriety, but Darcy found himself bewitched by her fine, bulbous eyes.

By the time the sisters left Netherfield the following week, Jane and Bingley were firmly in love, and Darcy was quite nose-over-paws for Elizabeth too – despite her inferior connexions, and her embarrassment of a mother, he simply could not repress his feelings. Elizabeth herself was glad to be away from him.

Soon the Bennet family had an unexpected guest – Mr Collins, their pompous clergypug cousin. His reason for visiting was unclear, but he seemed reluctant to leave a dismayed Elizabeth's side. 'I am happy on every occasion,' her cousin slobbered on her gallantly, 'to offer little delicate compliments which are always acceptable to bitches.'

One day, while the Bennets and Mr Collins were out for their walk, they were reacquainted with Wickham. He was certainly the most agreeable pug Elizabeth ever saw, of fine countenance and good figure. He told her he had been a ward of Darcy's father. Darcy had jealously deprived Wickham of his rightful inheritance when his father died, banishing him to poverty. Elizabeth was touched by Wickham's plight, and appalled that Darcy could be such a bad dog.

Elizabeth was thinking distractedly about Wickham that evening when she was ambushed with a proposal of marriage from Mr Collins: 'I must assure you in the most animated yapping of the violence of my affection,' he wheezed. Her repeated rejections only elicited praise for her feminine modesty, until she finally bounded out of the room. Mrs Bennet begged Elizabeth to reconsider, but she would not obey. Only love would persuade her to marry.

M r Collins wasn't too disheartened,
for within a few days he was engaged
to Elizabeth's best friend Charlotte (for
whom money was as good a reason as any for
matrimony).

It was on a visit to their parsonage home in
Kent that Elizabeth was once again forced to
cross paths with *that* abominable Darcy.

On the happy eve before Darcy was scheduled to leave the parsonage, Elizabeth was utterly amazed to be interrupted at her ruminations by none other than Darcy himself – who promptly proceeded to ask for her paw! It was against his will, reason and character, he woofed warmly, but he could not but love her.

He *spoke* of apprehension and anxiety, but his countenance expressed real security. So it must have been a shock when she growled, 'You are the last dog in the world whom I could ever be prevailed on to marry!'

Elizabeth upbraided Darcy for his arrogance and his reprehensible treatment of Wickham, until his infamous pride was mortified, and he hastily left the room. But before leaving the next day, he gave Elizabeth a letter. Within, he explained the truth about Wickham – he was a gamester, and had tried to elope with Darcy's sister when she was just a pup!

Elizabeth read the letter, and found her feelings for Darcy changing. 'How despicably have I acted!' she howled in shame. 'Till this moment, I never knew myself.'

Elizabeth passed the next few weeks in dull spirits, until her aunt and uncle, the Gardiners, invited her to join them on their northern tour. Elizabeth was very pleased to accept; perhaps this would take her mind off Darcy.

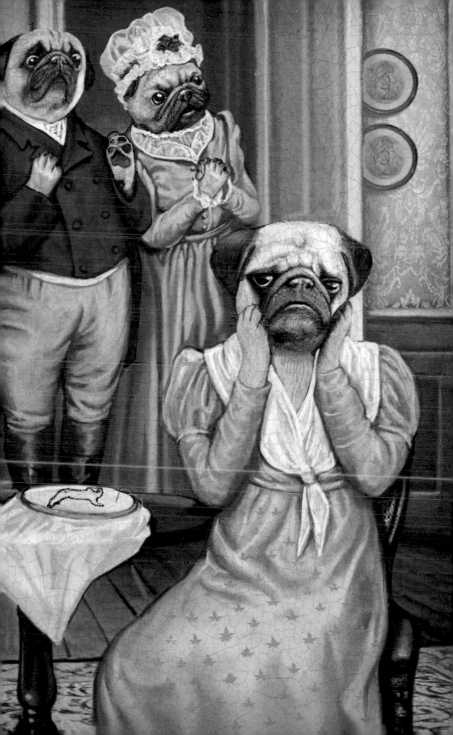

Or perhaps not. A short while into their tour, the group arrived in Derbyshire, and found themselves but a mile away from Darcy's Pemberley estate. Mrs Gardiner excitedly proposed a romp on the grounds.

Elizabeth was distressed at the plan, until she discovered that the Darcys were away for the summer. To Pemberley, therefore, they would go.

Driving through the great estate, Elizabeth was struck by the beauty and elegance of her surroundings. She could see Darcy's taste in every aspect, and thought of what could have been — to be mistress of Pemberley might be something!

The group were taken on a tour by Darcy's adoring housekeeper, who told them of his great generosity and goodness as they padded through the grand house.

'If I was to go through the world, I could not meet with a better master,' she puffed.

Can this be Mr Darcy? thought Elizabeth.

They left the housekeeper and began to cross the lawn, when suddenly they were met by Darcy, just shaking himself off after a paddle in the lake. Elizabeth was mortified – how strange it must appear to him, her being there! But he was perfectly civil, and as their eyes met, he thought her the handsomest beast of his acquaintance.

They did not have long to reacquaint themselves, for soon a letter arrived for Elizabeth bearing terrible news. Her flighty younger sister Lydia had eloped – with none other than the scoundrel Wickham!

'She is lost for ever!' Elizabeth whimpered to Darcy, and fled Pemberley in grief and disgrace.

There followed a time of tense waiting while attempts were made to remedy this sad affair. Eventually news reached the Bennets that Wickham had agreed to marry Lydia! Elizabeth was relieved (and Mrs Bennet overjoyed), but she couldn't fathom it. The Bennets had no money to pay him, so what could have brought him to do the right thing?

The answer was revealed when a smug newly-wed Lydia visited her family home, and let slip that Darcy had been at their wedding. Elizabeth soon discovered that Darcy had paid off Wickham's considerable debts on the condition that he marry Lydia. Elizabeth was stunned. Could he have done this for *her*?

Soon happier times befell Longbone, as Bingley finally proposed to his beloved Jane. 'I am certainly the most fortunate creature that ever existed!' cried Jane that night. 'Oh Lizzy, if I could but see *you* as happy!'

Darcy joined Bingley on his next visit to Longbone, and Elizabeth had the opportunity to thank him for what he had done for her family.

'Your family owe me nothing. Much as I respect them, I believe I thought only of you.'

This time, Elizabeth did not reject Darcy's proposal.

Mr Bennet was shocked at the news, and a little suspicious. 'He is rich, to be sure. But will that make you happy?'

'I love him,' was her solemn response.

'If that be the case, he deserves you. I could not have parted with you, my Lizzy, to anyone less worthy.'

With the blessing of Mr Bennet, the happy couple were wed. 'Dearest Elizabeth,' Darcy dribbled tenderly. 'You must allow me to tell you how ardently I admire and love you!'

'I am the happiest creature in the world!' she snuffled in reply.

THE END

First published in 2017 by WILDFIRE
an imprint of HEADLINE PUBLISHING GROUP

Illustrations copyright © Bob Venables

1

Cataloguing in Publication Data is available from the British Library

ISBN 978 1 4722 4977 7

Written by Eliza Garrett

Typeset in Perpetua

Printed and bound in Portugal by Printer Portuguesa

HEADLINE PUBLISHING GROUP
An Hachette UK Company
Carmelite House
50 Victoria Embankment
London EC4Y 0DZ

www.headline.co.uk
www.hachette.co.uk